Rev. & Mrs. James Witt
526 N Willson St
Blue Hill, NE 68930

What Is Not Seen

By Diana Montanez-Mendoza

Diana M.M.

CreateSpace

Copyright © 2013 by Diana Montanez-Mendoza

All rights reserved. This book or any portion thereof

may not be reproduced or used in any manner whatsoever

without the express written permission of the publisher

except for the use of brief quotations in a book review.

Printed in the United States of America

First Printing, 2013

ISBN 978-1492148555

Diana Montanez-Mendoza

216 West 21 St.

Grand Island, NE 68801

www.createspace.com

For our struggle is not against flesh and blood, but against the rulers, against the authorities, against the powers of this dark world and against the spiritual forces of evil in the heavenly realms.

                    Ephesians 6:12 (NIV)

Chapter 1

Monsters of darkness. Destroyers of light. Creatures that fed on earthly souls. Fallen angels of sin and evil. Demons.

Demons were hunting a thirteen year old boy named Oliver Ravensdale.

I ran through the dense mist that entangled the forest. I tripped over large roots while scrawny tree branches clawed at me, yet I ran as fast as I possibly could.

Had I been running for an eternity? Those monsters could easily catch up to me, but I was confident that they enjoyed seeing my useless struggles.

The monsters. I had gotten a good view of them when they had first surrounded me. They were repulsive! They truly had no equal in the best of horror movies. They were the exact opposite of angelical.

Cruel smiles, angry eyes, an aura of death and suffering. Each beast was bloodied and broken in its own way. Some had missing eyes and jaws that hung down to their chests. Some had broken bones protruding from their skin or rotting flesh. Meanwhile others had skinless bodies and intestines hanging out. I only listed a few examples.

Since I first laid eyes on them, I had never looked back. I just ran. Still I wanted to know exactly how close they were to me.

I glanced back hurriedly and my heart raced in fear. They were less than an arm's length away!

I forgot to look forward. That caused me to stumble over a tree root. I plummeted to the ground, landing face down. My chest ached and I could feel blood leaking from my elbows and knees.

I lay there as I felt them hover me. I had no idea what had led up to this.

I knew that soon, these things would kill me. I just wanted to know why they wanted to kill me so badly. So I asked them.

A large clawed hand lifted me by the collar of my shirt. I saw its face and felt the need to vomit. My captor had a nearly decapitated head, broken ribs, and skinless, rotting flesh. "Your soul is quite the treasure. We'll destroy your physical body, and take it."

I screamed as the brute pulled back a muscled, skinless arm with sharpened black talons as though he were to impale me straight through the chest.

Suddenly I felt nothing and blacked out.

Chapter 2

I awoke with a start. Where was I? I sat there hyperventilating for a few minutes. To my great relief, I realized that I was in my room, and had suffered from another nightmare.

The digital alarm clock on my nightstand said that it was 4:36 A. M. Outside it was still dark and not a sound was heard throughout the house.

I lay back down. I closed my eyes and thought about the bad dream. It wasn't the first time that I had had it. It had repeatedly visited me for almost a month. I didn't know why though. Perhaps it had been caused by listening to my friend Richard's ghost stories. That was most likely the reason.

Still, as I drifted off to sleep, something told me that it was more than just a lowly nightmare.

Birds sang and the commotion of people rang up from downstairs. Sunlight streamed in through the thin blue curtains of my room, giving off an aqua lighting.

I sat up yawning. It was nice that I managed to catch some sleep after waking up so early.

I got up and dressed myself in a gray t-shirt and black sweat pants. I got frightened when I saw that it was 9:12 on a Monday, but relaxed when I remembered that it was summer vacation.

Briskly I went across the hall into the bathroom. Before I left, I paused in front of the mirror and gazed at my reflection. Tall and lanky, pale with light blonde hair, all were traits belonging to my father. My gray eyes were entirely my mother's.

I went downstairs and headed into the kitchen. No one was there but a fresh pile of dishes in the sink.

Next I tried the living room. There I found my two siblings, Arthur and Samantha. Arthur, the oldest, was busy on his smartphone, while the youngest, Samantha, watched kid cartoons.

Our parents were working for the day, so we were home alone.

Arthur noticed me standing in the entryway. "It took you long enough to wake up."

I responded, "There wasn't any need to get up early."

"Actually there was, but you're up now so I've got a favor to ask you, Oliver." He stood up, revealing that he was dressed for exercise. "I need to go on my daily run. Just 'cause it's summer doesn't mean that I'll slack off."

I should have expected that. Arthur was the athlete of the family and a valuable member of most every sports team at his high school.

Since he'd be out running, I would have to take care of our little sister. "What will I get for watching Samantha?"

"I'll let you run off with your friends whenever you want to." Arthur grabbed his keys and left, closing the door with a thud.

He knew that I couldn't resist that offer. If I babysat Samantha for him, he'd do the same for me.

Samantha looked up from the TV and her stuffed pony and smiled at me. "You're nicer than Art is."

I laughed and went into the kitchen. Samantha was kind and sweet, but too girly for me to enjoy her company. Eventually she would only succeed in annoying me.

I had sat down to eat a bowl of cereal when my old flip phone lit up with a text.

It was from Richard. The message read:

Meet me at 10:30 at my house so that we can head over to Ed's house. I've got to show you guys something awesome!

Well, that couldn't be good. Anytime Richard wanted to show us something or do something, we'd get in some sort of trouble. Once we got locked inside a walk-in freezer for a few hours, until a surprised employee found us.

Still, whatever he had planned was better than spending the day cooped up with my brother and sister.

I sent back a message that I would go. Besides, Richard's antics had never been life threatening, so what did I have to lose?

I finished my breakfast and then I joined Samantha in the living room with a book.

After about half an hour, Arthur returned. He was drenched in sweat and appeared to be ready to pass out.

"Out of shape, eh?"

He scowled. "In better shape than you'll ever be, kid."

Arthur was right about that. I wasn't athletic at all. To be honest, I didn't like sports. I failed at every single one.

"I'm gonna take a shower," said Arthur. "Keep an eye on Sammy for another while."

Curse him. I was stuck once more reading *Dracula* to the tune of *My Little Ponies*.

With a sigh I continued to read. In my opinion, the Count was an idiot. Surely he would've thought that someone would try to stop him. Sadly he never counted on Dr. Van Helsing to be an expert on vampires.

It was a good thing that this was only fiction. I'm pretty sure that we'd all be living in terror if vampires and others of their kind were real.

Another thirty minutes passed. I was all ready to leave, and my phone kept ringing from the messages telling me to hurry.

Finally Arthur bounded down the stairs. "So, where are you going?"

I opened the door and answered, "I'm going to a friend's house."

"Alright. Be back by the time Mom gets home."

I proceeded to walk next door to a bright yellow house, belonging to Richard's family. His mother answered the door. "Hi there, Oliver! Rich will be out in just a moment."

Soon enough Richard was at the door with his ever present grin slightly wider than usual. "Hey! Let's go!"

"Keep yourselves safe, okay?" called his mother.

Richard replied, "We'll be safe."

He and I walked together to our other friend Edward's house. He lived out in the countryside close to the forest that surrounded our town like a green wall.

I asked Richard, "What do you want to show us?"

"It's a surprise."

"You'd better not get us in trouble this time."

He laughed at me. "I won't."

I kept on walking with Richard and felt a feeling of dread. The mischief in Richard's eyes and the rectangle shape in the sack he carried told me that no matter what he said, something bad was going to happen.

Chapter 3

After twenty minutes of walking, we made it to Edward's house. A large, two-story, sky blue, inviting place.

We knocked on the door and it was immediately opened by Mrs. Jones, Edward's mother.

"Hello, boys!" She stood aside. "Ed is in his room. If you two need anything, I'll be in the kitchen!"

Richard and I nodded and headed upstairs. I was extremely familiar with Edward's home. I usually spent as much time here as I spent at my own house.

Edward's door was wide open and he was sitting in a chair expecting us. "Hi," he said groggily, since he had most likely been interrupted in his plans to sleep until late in the afternoon.

"So...?" I asked Richard expectantly.

Unfortunately, he wasn't very quick to understand.

"Aren't you going to show us your *great* surprise?" clarified Edward.

"Oh, right." He adjusted his bag awkwardly. "I have to show you somewhere private."

Strange. "Couldn't we just close the door?" I suggested.

"Nah, it's not really approp- I mean private enough here." Richard paused for a moment before he spoke again. "Why don't we go out into the woods?"

Edward seemed uneasy about it. "I don't know, but I'll ask my mom."

"What's in that bag that we have to go into the forest? I swear, Rich, one of these days you're going to kill us!"

Richard was amused at my discomfort. "Are you scared, Olly?"

I crossed my arms in defiance. "No, I'm not scared at all! I'm just not in the mood for your little games."

It was a poor cover up, and we both knew it.

Thankfully, Edward returned and I was saved from any further mockery. "We can go...we'll just have to be back around noon."

"Alright!" shouted Richard as he ran downstairs.

I exchanged a nervous glance with Edward as we followed him out into the backyard. There was only a fence separating us from the forest. I had only been in there one time, along time ago, and I only remembered it as being dark.

It was also then that I recalled my ever present nightmare. It was set in a forest! What if...no. I was being paranoid.

"Aren't you coming?" Richard called out to me. He and Edward were standing outside the gate.

I pushed back my worries and followed them, feeling a little like a sheep being led to a sacrificial altar.

The forest wasn't as dark as I had thought it would have been, but it still had poor lighting. There was a dampness in the air that clung to one's body. Every once in awhile a bird sang, or small animal scurried along, and there was the constant noise of a woodpecker.

Our trio kept to the beaten path that ran in between the trees. Richard stopped us once we were deep into the forest. We stood where trees grew sparsely and above, gray clouds were collecting and soon we knew that it would rain.

"What did you have to show us, Richard?" asked Edward.

"You'll see," said he. Richard set down his bag, unzipped it, and pulled out an Ouija board.

Edward freaked out. "What the heck?! No wonder that you didn't show us at my house! Are you crazy!"

I didn't care very much about the Ouija board, I simply wondered where he had gotten it from. But Edward came from a devout Christian family, so I could understand why he was frightened.

"Calm down," said Richard. "It's only a harmless game. It's rigged to act like a ghost is there, because we all know that spirits aren't real."

Honestly I couldn't believe that Richard said that. We tried to avoid topics on religion and entities since Edward was the only Christian and we didn't want anyone getting butt hurt feelings, but Richard seemed to forget quite often.

Edward huffed. "I believe in them! What if you summon an angry ghost, or even a demon?"

Richard sighed in exasperation. "Listen, the game works with two people, so you don't have to play."

"Fine." Edward walked away from us and sat under a tree, yet he still faced us to see what would happen.

So in the end it rested on me. I didn't believe in the nonsense of the paranormal, and if I humored Richard, then we could leave the forest faster. "Alright, I'll play."

"Awesome!"

We sat across from each other and placed the board on our laps. "I'll ask the questions," said Richard.

"Who taught you to play?" I asked.

"My sister did. She let me borrow it to show you guys."

Ha, more like he stole it from her room.

He continued, "Put your fingers on the pointer. Now, we move it in a circle."

We did that for a minute or two, until Richard said that it had been enough. "Any entities hanging around are welcome."

I was certain that this was a waste of time. Nothing was going to happen.

"Is anyone here?" inquired Richard.

Slowly, we got an answer. It said, "Yes."

"Thanks for coming!" Richard told the board.

Surely this had to be rigged.

"Are you a ghost?"

It answered, "No."

With a mischievous glance towards Edward, he asked, "Are you a demon?"

The board answered, "Yes."

I admit that the answer slightly spooked me, but this game was made to scare.

Richard asked it, "What do you want?"

The board said, "His soul."

"Who's soul?"

It answered bluntly, "Oliver's."

All of a sudden, I felt a choking sensation as though I was being strangled. This was too much. It sounded a little like the dream where those monsters chased me for my 'soul'. To Richard I said, "Stop the session."

I was ignored, since Richard was having fun with the Ouija board. "Too bad you can't have his soul, right?"

Nothing happened on the board.

"If you're real and you really want Oliver's soul, show yourself!"

I could hear Edward whimper in fear. I looked at him to see him fold his hands over the crucifix he wore. "What did you do?" He yelled at Richard.

"Relax," said Richard. "Nothing happened! You don't honestly think that some demon is out to get Oliver?"

I said nothing. The game was not real, I was simply paranoid from the nightmares. That had to be it.

"Oh my God..." Edward exclaimed in fear. He was staring wide eyed at something behind us.

Richard noticed too. We turned our heads to see a black mass taking form into something slightly humanoid.

"Is this enough proof for you, boy?" said a massive and skinless creature.

My heart nearly stopped. These were the things from my dreams, and Richard had just called them into reality.

Chapter 4

Richard and Edward took off running. A split second later I was on the run as well.

A heavy fog had settled in. I ran out from the path and into the mess of trees.

I could hear the demons laughing at my attempt to get away. They were just as monstrous as I had dreamed them to be.

I was certain of death. I wasn't fast enough to outrun the demons, but only now did I regret not being athletic.

How close were they? Had I lost them? I couldn't hear their laughter and scorn anymore. What were they planning? I had to know.

With haste, I turned my head and found myself looking into the coal black eyes of a demon.

I cried out and fell to the floor, scraping my elbows and knees. I knew only too well what came next.

A large, gnarled hand picked me up and held me above the ground. It was the near decapitated, skinless brute. "We finally meet face to face, Oliver Ravensdale."

Its breath smelled of a dying fish. I asked it timidly, "A-are you going to kill me...?"

That earned a laugh from the hellish legion. A bloated, feminine demon spoke up. "Your body shall perish, but your soul shall be a treasure in hell!"

It received a roar of approval from the other demons.

I didn't know what to do. It was all so terrifying and confusing. My mind wanted to shut down out of pure terror. Until now I had thought that demons belonged in horror stories and that souls didn't actually exist. Curse Richard and his sister's retarded board!

The demon that held me smiled a wicked grin and pulled back its sharpened, black claws. I felt faint.

The claws flew straight towards my heart and I anticipated it to pierce me. It never came. Instead I fell to the ground while my captor screeched in pain.

Its fellow demons disappeared in a hurry. I felt blackness creeping in from the corner of my eyes.

The last thing I saw before I passed out was a tall figure in a hooded, black coat smiling down at me.

Chapter 5

Dazedly, I opened my eyes. First I noticed that the ceiling was black. Then I saw that the bed I was in was white, and not my own.

I jumped out from under the covers and tried to figure out where in the world I was. I still wore my own sweaty clothing, but my knees and elbows had been bandaged.

The room I was in possessed a refined, dark Gothic look. It was most certainly elegant.

I forced myself to quit admiring my strange environment and headed to the door. Wherever I was, it wasn't home.

As my hand went to the door knob, it burst open, narrowly missing my face. A tall, raven haired man stood in front of me.

"You are awake, Mr. Ravensdale!" said he in a Romanian accent.

Who the heck was he? Had I been kidnapped? I needed to get out of that place, but I didn't know how.

The man bowed. "I am Stefan Desmodus, servant of Death. I mean you no harm, but instead protection."

Servant of Death, and protection from what? This Stefan Desmodus must be crazy!

"Come with me," he said. "I shall take you to one who is able to answer the many questions possibly running through your little head."

I had no idea of where I was, and I did not trust this man at all, I hadn't even talked to him once, but I wanted to know where I was, and what I was doing there. "Uh, sure."

"Follow me, Mr. Ravensdale."

Stefan led me down a long hallway, lined with alternating black and white doors. We entered an elevator and headed for the top floor.

There was an awkward silence. It was quiet, and I couldn't hear anything but my own breathing. I asked Stefan, "Who am I going to talk to?"

He ran his fingers through his hair. "The Angel of Death."

"But angels don't exist."

Stefan fixed his purple eyes with strange golden specks on me in disbelief. "Even after encountering the demons, you doubt angels' existence?"

"I could be having a lucid dream," I said looking down at my muddy sneakers.

"What a lucid dream indeed!"

The elevator came to a stop and we stood before two, big, ebony doors with a skull knocker.

Stefan lightly tapped the door a few times, and the door swung open. He pushed me inside and whispered in my ear, "I shall come for you when you have finished."

I was left standing in the middle of the luxurious office with large pillars connecting the floor to the ceiling. A desk towards the back had a black book on it, two swivel chairs, and realistic paintings of different parts of the world.

A sudden white light flashed in the room, and the person that I had seen previous to my fainting was seated at the desk, flipping through the book. He had snow white hair and porcelain like skin, and he still wore the black hooded robe.

He looked up at me. "Oliver James Ravensdale. Born July 26th, 2000 to Michael and Eloise Ravensdale. Death," he smiled. "I cannot reveal."

I stood there, dumbfounded. All of this information from a book. I had been right, this simply was another dream. All the previous ones had been as realistic as this one.

The man continued to flip the pages of the book and made no move to speak to me. I then remembered what Stefan Desmodus had said. "So, are you the Angel of Death?"

He stood to show that he was about the size of a tall basketball player. "Yes, I am the Angel of Death," The 'angel' bowed to me, "servant of God Almighty."

I decided to ignore his claim to be a servant of a god. I didn't think that there was any use arguing with these people. It wouldn't solve anything at all. Instead I asked about how he had known my birthday, full name, and parents, and why he had said he knew when I would die.

The Angel of Death patted the black book fondly. "You are currently in the Book of Life, like every living thing since creation."

"Oh, I see." In reality, I did not see. Everything that had happened was confusing to me.

Death sat back down and motioned for me to sit across from him. "God sent me to save you from those demons, since you did not directly summon them. You are not the first to find yourself in a similar situation. It only happens when a door is opened to your dimension, and the demons are being summoned."

"How exactly were they summoned?"

"When Richard Stevenson told the demons to prove that they existed, the door was opened wide for the demons to pass through, and they had been trying to get to you."

I felt regret for playing the Ouija board with Rich. I wouldn't have found myself in this terrible situation if I had followed Edward. Still, it didn't explain why all those dreams kept tormenting me, night after sleepless night.

"Would you know how to explain why I have had dreams about being hunted by demons recently?"

"Demons," explained Death, "have only one mission, and that is to take as many human souls to Hell as possible. Sometimes, they don't have to work hard, the humans do most of the work by denying the faith, but other times they need to be more forceful. Demons at times sense when a soul has special potential to bring souls into the dark pits of hell, but they need to find a way to keep that soul under their influence. The way to do that is to form a contract, and that way the human can never be free.

"The demons wish to form a contract with you, but you would never involve yourself in such activities as you do not believe in them. They attempted to convince you to believe in them by invading your dreams, and that never worked. When you finally did partake in such an activity, the demons lunged at the chance. They would kill your physical body but keep you alive spiritually so that they would be able to transport you to hell, and once the contract was formed, your body would be brought back to life," finished Death with a smile. "You never wanted this, and God never allows demons to force a human into eternal damnation, so as usual when this sort of situation arises, I was sent for you."

None of this could be real! There wasn't any way this sort of thing was even remotely possible. I didn't know what to do, and I was terrified.

My fear must have shown in my expression for Death said to me, "Do not worry for I and my helpers shall protect you. No innocent mortal shall fall into the hands of Satan against his will."

Did he not know that I didn't believe in this nonsense? There is no God or no Satan, no angels or demons, no Heaven or Hell. "I'm sorry, but I'm an Atheist."

"I know, boy, we are well aware of your belief. I am not telling you to believe in God, that is your choice, simply listen to what we say so that you may remain safe until the demons no longer pursue you."

I sighed. "Fair enough then." It didn't matter because I would wake up eventually. "When will I be able to return home?"

"You shall not return to your earthly home until the demons have been dealt with."

"How long will that be? If this is actually happening, my parents will freak out."

"Do not worry, for you are in another dimension, one called the Other Realm, which has been mistaken as a purgatory or limbo by our past human visitors. Here time flows differently. A day in the Other Realm is merely a second on Earth."

"So like, if I spent six days in this place, back on Earth it would've only been six seconds?"

"Indeed."

That was one less thing for me to worry about. No one would be wondering where I was, and I wouldn't have to explain myself. I still wanted to know one thing. Who would protect me from those demons? I already knew that I couldn't defend myself at all.

The Angel of Death seemed to have read my mind. "In every case like yours, I assign a group of five of my good helpers to assist and defend you. Four of them are currently busy. You have already met one."

"Stefan Desmodus?"

"That is the one," confirmed Death. "The rest are some of the younger Grim Reapers, Matthias Asther, Sumiko Wakahisa, Anthony Griffin, and Luna Cortez-Valencia."

They seemed like a diverse bunch, and I hoped that they could actually do something besides run and scream like me. Death had said that they were Grim Reapers, and I had heard of the Grim Reaper. What exactly were Grim Reapers then? "Could you explain Grim Reapers?" I asked.

"Grim Reapers," started Death, "are beings who were once human, died in some unnatural way, and if they were chosen ones, would become collectors of souls. They know better than anyone how to keep an eye on a human in a life or death situation."

It felt a little strange to think that I was going to be watched, but at least the four Grim Reapers wouldn't try to kill me. Stefan seemed friendly enough.

"Any more questions, Oliver?"

"No, I have none left." In reality I had more questions, but I did not voice them. I preferred to find out later instead of being under this angel's scrutinizing eyes that looked like fireballs.

"In that case, Stefan will come for you now." He did nothing, he sat in his chair. In less than five seconds, Stefan came in.

"Come with me, Mr Ravensdale," said Stefan. "I am to give you a tour of our wondrous home, and few mortals have laid eyes on it."

I stood and followed him out, and was shocked to find that the Angel of Death had disappeared from the room. Where he once sat, there was only nothing.

Chapter 6

Stefan led me outside, and I noticed people of all kinds walking past with lists in their hands, and they all looked at me weirdly.

I stood outside of the building and for the first time saw how it looked. It appeared like a large, Gothic cathedral, with weeping angels perched where gargoyles were normally found. Church-like buildings surrounded it in a circle formation. Stefan explained that those served as apartments for the Grim Reapers.

"This land you see is called Soul Haven, headquarters of the Angel of Death."

On the outside of the circle were seven smaller buildings that resembled funerary homes.

Stefan said, "Grim Reapers go to those places to receive lists of souls that they are to collect daily. Each structure represents one of the seven continents."

Aside from the structures, there wasn't much to see. The sky was dark and dreary like it was before a rain shower. Paved sidewalks connected everything, and dark green grass ran alongside it.

The buildings that looked like churches had stained windows that depicted various Biblical scenes that I recognized because of Edward's family. Regardless of the Christian themes, it was nice art.

From there, Stefan took me on a road to another place. When we arrived I saw various styled homes from many different periods, such as the Victorian or Medieval times, even ancient Greek. The sky was like any other, and looked like early morning. The plants there were green and full of life. Yet a strange stench of decay permeated the air.

"Welcome to my home, Mr. Ravensdale! Vampire Coven."

"Vampire? Does that mean that you're a vampire?"

He laughed. "Hahaha, yes I am a vampire. You can always tell because of our violet or blue eyes with yellow specks."

"Why violet or blue with yellow specks?" I asked.

"All the better to hypnotize you weak-minded humans."

"I see." I didn't really find Stefan friendly and less likely to kill me anymore. I bet that if he got the chance, he'd bite me. Beside that, I was in a place full of blood suckers. When would this nightmare end?

The blood sucker that stood next to me remained oblivious to my discomfort and pulled out a key. "No matter how all of these houses appear, on the inside they are all the same."

I held back from following Stefan. I asked him, "You aren't going to drink my blood, right?"

Stefan went to a dark Victorian house and opened the door. "I was ordered to protect you, Mr. Ravensdale. Therefor I cannot hurt you in any way. Aside from those reasons, I am not hungry."

"Good." I slowly made my way into the house. A man who was deathly pale closed the door behind me. He moved sluggishly, almost like a robot.

Stefan spoke to the man. "Lewis, allow none to enter while our guest is here."

Lewis bowed and shuffled out to stand guard in front of the door.

"Is he a vampire?" I asked.

"No," Stefan answered. "Lewis is a ghoul."

We continued down a hallway and at the end there was a heavily locked door.

While Stefan unlocked it, I asked him about what a ghoul was.

"Ghouls were once human but they had all their blood drunk and they died. If a vampire chooses, they can revive the bodies of prey so that they may become eternal slaves. They cause less trouble than subordinate vampires, who may rebel and plot to end your existence."

I shuddered and felt sympathy for Lewis the ghoul. The poor man had been a meal for bloodthirsty Stefan and now had to be a slave for him. I regarded Stefan with more caution, not trusting his word to not hurt me.

The door came open. The room was empty, until at the far end I saw a coffin.

"This is the one of the only rooms in a vampire's home. Our tomb where we lay in our sleep."

"Don't vampires sleep during the day?"

Stefan scoffed at me. "That is a stereotype. We sleep whenever we feel like it."

"But doesn't the sun hurt you?"

He sighed. "That is only myth. It is simply easier to hunt at night than in day time."

That made me wonder about what else could be fake about these monsters. Only to irritate him I asked, "Well, do you sparkle in day time?"

Stefan bared his fangs. "Did you see me sparkle outside with the sun blazing overhead?!"

"No..."

"Exactly! Vampires do not sparkle."

"I was just wondering."

He straightened his long sleeved, white shirt. "We vampires simply aren't feared and respected these days." He herded me out the door. "Time to go, Mr. Ravensdale."

At the entrance, Lewis stood against a few vampires who had a wild look in their eyes.

"I smell a human!"

"Young blood too!"

"He smells divine!"

"I'm so hungry!"

Stefan acted as my shield and attempted to make them all leave. "The boy is under my protection! Back off!"

The vampires started to get rowdy when a stocky brunette man broke through the crowd. Everything got quiet.

The man asked, "What's going on?"

"Master," started Stefan as he bowed. "I was ordered by the Angel of Death to show this young human the Other Realm, and our respectable coven, when our brethren start acting uncivilized and tried to feed off of him."

The 'Master' hissed at the other vampires to leave and they hurriedly did so. He turned to us. "Desmodus, you never tell me when you are about to bring a human! Be sure to do so next time. You are fortunate that a relatively small number detected the boy." He walked away and called back, "Give Death my apologies."

Thankfully there were no more vampires sniffing out my blood. "Who was that man?" I asked.

"John Brown, our esteemed leader."

"I see."

Stefan ushered me out of Vampire Coven and relaxed once we were a fair distance away. "Next, I shall take you to the Were Lands. Hooray."

"Is someone going to try to eat me there?"

"Highly unlikely, Mr. Ravensdale."

We walked quickly as the sun rose higher into the sky. The grass started to become more wild and weeds sprouted up. Soon we came upon various animals, such as squirrels, rabbits, and other small mammals.

I watched a chipmunk that sat on a log, and then morphed into a human! An elderly man sat in his place.

"How did that happen?" I questioned.

"It is a Therianthrope, or a human that can shape shift into an animal. These lands are crawling with such beings."

"So it has things like werewolves?"

"Just like them, except with many kinds of animals."

I also saw a swan turn into a woman, and a fox turn into a boy. Eventually we started to travel through a meadow and entered a woodland area.

I heard wolves howling in the distance. An owl glanced at us inquisitively. Stefan began to lead me into it and said, "Be careful here. No need to frighten any werewolf by being loud and disorderly."

Light filtered down from the trees leaving the ground dotted with little spots. Bright flowers covered the ground. Unlike the forest back home, this one had a warm and secure feeling.

Out of nowhere, a tawny wolf jumped out in front of us. It morphed into a blonde teenage girl. "You are intruding upon our land. What is your reason, undead monster!"

Stefan produced a skull the size of an apple -speaking of apples I had started to get hungry- and he answered the girl. "I am here by command of the Angel of Death. There is no need to get overprotective, for I come to show this poor human your beloved home."

The girl looked at me curiously. "So that's the boy the demons want?"

How the heck did she know? "You've heard?" I asked her.

"News travels fast, especially since there's a very good gossip among the Reapers."

Stefan scowled. "I'll have a talk with Anastasia about leaking information..."

The tall girl sighed. "Too bad that Alpha doesn't have an excuse to cut off your head and drain your body of blood, vampire! I'll tell him you aren't a threat."

"What's your name? I have to fill out a report later about any obstacles I encountered," said Stefan.

"It's April Padalecki," she started to morph back into a wolf, "and don't think that we won't be keeping an eye you."

I guessed that werewolves and vampires weren't so friendly towards one another. Stefan moved on. "Let us continue before another mutt gets in our way, Mr. Ravensdale."

I ran to catch up to him. "Why was April Padalecki so mean to you? Have you two met before?"

Stefan shook his head. "No, I have never met that young one. Thousands of years ago, there was a bloody war between our races. These dogs know how to hold grudges, even to the point of passing them to their young, like you saw in that girl."

A war had occurred between vampires and werewolves, and I must admit that that sounded pretty awesome. This Other Realm sure was an interesting place with its own history. This had to be the most intriguing dream I had ever had.

The woods gave way into picturesque gardens. Green life-filled plants were everywhere, spring and summer flowers grew in large groups, and pathways led around magnificent water fountains. Stone statues of people, angels, and animals were meticulously placed throughout.

"We have entered Fairy Village, where you may find elves, gnomes, pixies, dwarves, goblins, and other strange little folk," announced Stefan.

I found it very funny that after passing through places with Grim Reapers, vampires, and werewolves, you'd encounter fairies. It made no sense, and only proved that none of this was real.

"Yeah, well I don't see any fairies around here-"

I was cut off by a sharp kick to my shin. It had been delivered by a short old man about three feet tall. He had a large, white beard to complete his appearance.

"What was that for?!" I yelled.

He shook his fist at us. "Get outta my garden, idiots! Don't ya respect private property?"

Stefan lowered himself to be eye level with the midget. "Don't touch the boy, he is under divine protection. Also, this land belongs to every creature. Only your houses are 'private property', so we have every right to be here."

The old man slapped his thigh in agitation. "Oh, gosh darn it! You people respect nothing!" He then hobbled off into the bushes.

Stefan kept walking and I followed once more. I was also getting really hungry, but where would I get food?

I decided to ignore my hunger and asked about the old man.

"That was a gnome," explained Stefan. "Crazy, greedy little things."

In that case, that had been a strange old gnome. I hoped that another wouldn't pop up and kick me elsewhere.

Despite what Death had said, I was worried about meeting the demons again somewhere. I missed my home, my friends and family. Why could I not wake up and see real life?

Further into the elaborate gardens, hummingbirds zipped around. Stefan said that they were not hummingbirds, but pixies.

At a closer look, I realized that they were not flying, but actually jumping at incredible speeds. They rarely stopped, and when one did, I saw that it was childlike and dressed in rags.

A few of them came close to us and whispered excitedly. One pointed to the crimson ribbon that tied Stefan's hair back. They attempted to jump up and get it, but came short at his shoulders.

The vampire chuckled. "I always lose a ribbon coming through here!" He threw it to the pixies. "Now they shall fight over it, and won't try to lead us astray."

Sure enough, a little pixie mob was brawling for the ribbon. I would've hated to have been there when it was torn to pieces.

We went around the mob and didn't look back. I looked up into the bright, blue sky, reminded of how hungry I was. I really hoped that there was food in this place.

Gigantic mushrooms sprouted up ahead. Houses were built into the colorful toadstools. Small people dressed like medieval commoners ran around, completing chores like laundry or harvesting from little patches of soil.

Some of them eyed us curiously, but most were too focused on their work. Tiny versions of them, I guessed their children, helped out or played outdoor games like hopscotch and jump rope.

Stefan and I observed them from a distance. "Those are elves," said Stefan. "Hardworking creatures. When they aren't busy here, they like to secretly help out you humans."

"What do they help with?"

"Finding lost things, keeping pets out of trouble, helping to keep human children out of danger. Things of the sort."

"That's nice."

"Indeed it is, Mr. Ravensdale."

Instead of walking through the mushrooms, where behind rose huge mountains, Stefan took me east of it.

I asked him, "Why aren't we going to the mountains? Is nothing there or what?"

"In those mountains there are many caves inhabited by little beasts that look like elves, but are more wicked and perverse. It is best to stay away from them, Mr. Ravensdale."

We stopped at a hole that seemed to be deeper than an abyss. Stefan dropped a rock down avoiding a ledge that jutted out inside. "Goblins populate the underground. Never go to the underground."

"Why not?"

"Would you like to have them feast upon your body? Come on, I'll push you in," said Stefan teasingly.

"No, no, I'm fine here," I said and took a few steps back.

"Then stay away."

"Yes, sir..."

Under all of this fairytale like wonders, lived evil man eating carnivores. How nice.

Each land we had gone to had a leader such as the Angel of Death, John Brown, or the Alpha, so this Fairy Village must have one as well. "Who's leader here?" I inquired while watching the ground for anymore holes.

"Morgan le Fay," answered Stefan as if it was normal.

I stopped in my tracks. "She's real?"

Stefan pushed me forward. "Yes, she is. Morgan le Fay was the one who started the King Arthur stories."

"I never thought that Morgan le Fay would be a fairy!"

"No," said Stefan, "she is a witch who sold her soul to live until Judgment Day and to be ruler of the fairy folk as well."

It was somewhat confusing to see the troubled and far away look on Stefan's face. I bet that he had something to do with Morgan, but I said nothing. I didn't want to anger the vampire a lot.

We began to approach a sizable body of water. The grass stopped short of the hot sand. Beyond the yellow sand was a deep blue ocean, that stretched on endlessly.

Stefan said that it was the home of mermaids and mermen, who lived deeper in the ocean. Occasionally they visited the shore, but not often.

A long screech brought my attention to the sky above. Harpies flew overhead, circling me like vultures.

There was nowhere to hide, since we were out in the open. I didn't want to die!

I couldn't believe Stefan! He was just standing there! Wasn't he supposed to protect me?!

The harpies started to swoop down lower so that I could feel the air from under their wings.

Something happened to the vampire man. His flesh rotted like a corpse. His fangs elongated from his mouth, his eyes glowed a terrible purple with cat-like pupils, and his nails grew to large claws. He let out a long hiss at the harpies, and they fled, still screeching. I had fallen to the ground out of fear and scooted away from the beast.

It laughed at me as it reverted to its more humane form. "Hahahaha! It is so amusing to see the fear in someone's face when they see me for who I am! Hahahaha!"

"How is it funny to scare people to death? I thought that those beasts were frightening, but you are the biggest monster of them all!" I shouted at Stefan.

He quit his laughter but still wore his smirk. He held out his hand so that he could help me up. "Mr. Ravensdale, I have no human emotions. I am not like you. I am truly, as you say, a monster."

I hesitantly took his hand and pulled myself to my feet. "Yeah, well it's confusing to me."

"There are many things in all of creation that mere men cannot fathom.

Now, let us go before those pests return."

Hurriedly we departed from the beach. Over the horizon, I could see large plains, and farther off many trees.

When we came closer, I heard the stampeding of hooves in the distance.

Stefan stopped me just when a herd of normal people rode by on horseback, and at a second glance at the figures I realized that there were no humans or horses, but centaurs.

A few spared us a passing glance but most galloped on.

While we waited for them to leave, Stefan asked me, "What do you think this area is home to?"

I thought hard. Mermaids lived in the ocean, harpies hung around the beach, and centaurs roamed the prairie. Each one had human features mixed with animal features. So the area must contain mythical hybrid creatures.

I answered, "Is this the place for hybrids?"

"Indeed it is, Mr. Ravensdale. And there remains one being that you have not seen."

"What is it?"

"It is a satyr."

A satyr? Like in Percy Jackson or Narnia? Yeah, none of this could have actually been real. It had to have been some random dream.

Stefan looked across the prairies and spoke to me. "The distance is great, and a small child such as yourself will never make it in a day's time. Allow me to carry you, Mr. Ravensdale."

"No, I'm not comfortable with that! I can run kinda fast. Wha-"

I had no room to finish my sentence because the vampire had become a humongous black bird and held me by grabbing my shirt.

I nearly died of fear at the high elevation at which I was held. The bird rose high into the air, and the ground below seemed almost like a golden quilt square. I had never been off the ground before, and now that I had I was ready to puke.

The bird's claws tore at my shirt for more cloth to grasp. I was sure that if we continued to fly over the land at alarming speeds, I would find myself a splatter upon the tall grass.

The prairies had ended, and now another forest began. The bird lowered itself and I was lightly deposited at a big tree. A cellar door was at the base of it.

The black bird turned back into Stefan, and he knocked on the door, and called, "Raymond the Satyr, it is your old acquaintance, Stefan Desmodus."

No one answered for a while. Stefan explained, "Satyrs are secretive and shy creatures, you must have patience with them."

The door was unlatched and a man's head popped out. He had red hair and a small beard and wore a green vest with Christmas trees. I could not tell what his bottom half looked like, for the man was half hidden in the tree's shadow.

"Hello, Raymond!" Stefan greeted him.

Raymond timidly stood from his cellar and returned the greeting. "Hello, Stefan. Why are you here?"

Stefan pointed to me, while I was occupied gawking at Raymond's goat legs and hooves. "I've brought Oliver Ravensdale to see a satyr for the first time."

The ginger satyr jumped, since he had not taken notice of me, but he gave me a sympathetic smile. "Poor kid. How scarring this whole ordeal must be for you! I fear for your soul's safety."

"Yeah, I guess," said I, not wanting to argue with them. The whole thing was just a dream. My 'soul' wasn't in any danger whatsoever.

"Well," said Stefan, his W's sounding like *V's*, "It is time for me to take the unfortunate boy back to the Soul Haven. He has seen a satyr, and that is all I came here for. Goodbye, Raymond."

Raymond laughed softly. "That's the old vampire I know. Straight to business as always."

My stomach growled loudly, causing Stefan to look at me quizzically. Raymond face palmed. "You're supposed to feed him, right?"

"Oh that is right. I forgot about that, haha!" Stefan muttered something to himself, and seemed a little agitated.

"Wait right here, Oliver," said Raymond to me. He dove back into his home and returned a few minutes later with a small slice of bread and an apple. "Take this and eat, or else you'll starve! Remind them that you are a growing kid."

"Thank you so much!" I smiled at the food I was now holding. I ate the bread first and felt my stomach calm its rage of hunger.

Raymond gently ruffled my hair. "If ever you need help, come to me. All of my brethren will eagerly assist you as well. Just say that you know me, Raymond Renault, their leader."

It surprised me that such a shy person was in charge of an entire group of creatures, but he was kind and generous, so in a way I could tell why too.

Stefan impatiently walked away. "Come on, boy! We must hurry back now."

I happily waved good bye to the charitable satyr. I hurried after the speed-walking undead.

It was hard to keep up with Stefan's fast pace. He was in some sort of haste and wouldn't even glance at me to make sure that I was there.

The trees lost their life and grew into a few sparse, dead ones. The sky was dark and stormy, and it dawned on me that we had returned to Soul Haven.

Stefan sped away into the cathedral, and I ran in behind him. Inside, he hurriedly conversed with a dark skinned teenager, and disappeared down a side hallway.

The boy laughed at the fleeing vampire. "I've never seen the old man run from a human!"

"Uh, why was he running from me?" I asked him.

He stretched his arms and answered me, "Well, you're a human, he's a vampire, he's hungry, you're a blood source. He's supposed to protect you, but if he was hungry he might have forgotten that."

"Oh." I feared Stefan even more than before, knowing that he could've drunk all of my blood at any moment.

"By the way," said the boy, "I'm Anthony Griffin."

Chapter 7

Anthony and I sat in a cafeteria where I was served a proper meal by a strange old woman with a blue nose that kept licking her lips.

We both got to know each other while I ate. I didn't have to say much, as Anthony already knew plenty. About him I learned that he was an African-American Grim Reaper, or helper of the Angel of Death, who had died at the age of sixteen.

He said that it had been awhile since the demons had gone so far for a human, the last time being the late 90's. "But don't worry too much, kid," said Anthony, "We'll put those devils in their place!"

After I finished, Anthony guided me back to my room, where we both sat in swivel chairs opposite each other.

For some time, nothing was said, and I had time to think in peace for the first time. I was in the strangest place, crawling with danger, and full of good people. It gave me a warm feeling to know that people were looking out for me, but I felt bad knowing that I couldn't do anything on my own.

Anthony broke the silence. "Well kid, I'm supposed to teach you about demons, but I don't know where to start. What do you want to know first?"

A part of me really didn't want to hear anymore about the demons. But another part wanted to be able to know more and not feel useless. "What exactly are demons?"

"Demons are fallen angels," said Anthony as though that was enough of an answer.

"Fallen angels?" I sheepishly asked.

"Fallen angels," continued the neon green-eyed Reaper, "used to be good angels that betrayed God and tried to take His power and Heaven, the ultimate dimension, but failed.

"So in shame, the traitors were banished to Earth," he finished.

I scoffed. "What a loving, forgiving God you have, right?"

Anthony frowned, but refrained from saying anything back to me about what I said. Instead, he said, "The Angel of Death has ordered us to respect your beliefs, but kid, it wouldn't hurt you to respect ours."

"I guess. Sorry," said I, although I really didn't care.

He shrugged. "Just a warning. Of the five of us that are on babysitting duty, only one has a pretty bad and defensive temper."

I asked, "Which one of you?"

"I'm not telling you, kid!" Anthony teased. "If I hear screams of anger or pain, I'll know that you haven't been all that respectful."

I groaned. This couldn't have gotten any more worse. I was stuck in a nightmare full of Jesus Freaks. I remembered Stefan, and what he had said about him not having human emotions. "Anthony, are vampires Christians too?"

"No," he answered. "Vampires are not at all Christian. Whether or not they were as humans, doesn't matter. Whatever heart they had died when they did."

"I see." That meant that Stefan couldn't have been the defensive one, and I knew that Anthony was kind of laid back. I would have to see about the other three.

"So," Anthony continued, "what else do you wanna know about?"

I thought for a moment. I then asked, "Why do the demons want my 'soul'? Why mine and not someone else's?"

Anthony scratched at his shaved head. "Well, that's kinda hard to explain. Ah, see souls to demons, are like jewels or money to humans. The more they've got, the more rich and respected they are. Got that?"

"Yes."

He kept going. "Well, you know how some diamonds are nice than others? Bigger, rare color, stuff like that?"

"Yeah, I know."

"To demons, souls are like that too. Each soul is unique, but some possess stronger traits of innocence, purity, courage, kindness, or intelligence.

Yours is like that, with many nice virtues. It makes it even more appealing because you're not a believer."

"So?" I asked, not seeing what this had to do with anything.

"So it makes you more of a prize to demons. If they got your soul, they'd be more respected among their demonic ranks."

That sucked. There was no way that these Grim Reapers could stop the demons. My dreams had been corrupted and I was certain that I had been traumatized. They wouldn't just go away. Why could I not just wake myself up from this horrid nightmare?

"Don't freak out," Anthony said, most likely sensing my mental panic attack. "We know better than anyone how to deal with demons!"

"Doesn't feel like it!" I nearly shouted. "If you really knew how to control them, none of this would be happening!"

"Everything happens for a reason, kid."

"That's the answer to everything!" I proclaimed sarcastically.

Anthony smiled. "You'll see, kid! Anymore questions?"

I had tired of speaking with this Reaper. He meant well, but the mood soured after my panic attack. "Isn't there something else to do besides talking to you?"

"Well, what do you want to do?"

"I don't know," I answered truthfully.

"Well...we have a library."

"I don't think that I could really focus on reading."

"There's the cafeteria."

"I just ate, Anthony."

"Ah, there's also the computer lab, I never use it."

"Can you take me there?"

"Sure, kid."

"My name's Oliver."

"Whatever, kid."

The computer lab was enormous. The walls were lined with the most ancient of computers to the newest models.

I sat myself down at a small laptop, while Anthony stood at the doorway, dozing off.

I had been watching some funny scare or prank videos to take my mind of grim topics, when an Indian man with pen and paper came in and handed Anthony a list.

He left the room continuing to write another list. Anthony crossed his arms and leaned against the wall. "Well kid, work never ends! I've gotta go and collect some dead people. A friend of mine will come to watch you."

He left, and for the first time since I had arrived in the Other Realm I was all alone, and it was nice.

I sat back into the wooden chair and closed my eyes. So much had happened, and I didn't understand any of it. None of it made sense in any way. I mean, this was the stuff of fiction, things that I had always known as make believe. The only reason I had to explain the situation was that I was having another lucid nightmare. I thought that when I woke up, I'd turn the dream into a novel, or maybe just publish it somewhere on the Internet.

I sat there, pondering all of this until I heard a person come in. The person was a seemingly young Asian girl with strange pink eyes.

I was disappointed that I could not have spent more alone time, but I stopped whining when I heard the girl's happy tone.

"Hi, Oliver!" she said. "My name is Sumiko Wakahisa, and I am one of the Grim Reapers that has been assigned to you."

"Nice to meet you, Sumiko," said I, returning my attention to the computer screen. If only I had had more time to myself, but I had a feeling that I was being watched regardless.

Sumiko spoke to me pitifully. "I'm so sorry about what you're going through. It must be so difficult for a young mind."

I shrugged. It truly wasn't something anyone could control. If someone could, we'd live in a perfect world.

"What are you watching?" Sumiko asked, attempting to make conversation.

"Pranks. Laughable stupidity."

"I really dislike those! I always feel bad for the people getting pranked. I should know, because Anthony pranks us all the time."

"I see," I said, not wanting to speak with anyone at the time.

Sensing that her attempt had failed, Sumiko pulled out an old tablet.

We remained that way in a heavy silence for a while. I wanted to say something, thinking that I had probably come off as harsh, but I said nothing. I wasn't going to become friends with people who weren't even real.

Sumiko abruptly stood and put her electronic away. She turned off the laptop I had been using me and told me to get up. "Come on, Oliver, there's something I better show you."

I was well aware that I followed her like a pouting little kid pulled away from the park. I didn't care, for I knew that Sumiko would pull me back into the grim events I had been trying to forget.

Along the winding hallways, various people trailed past with lists of some form in their hands. People from all nations, people resembling characters from myths and tales of the Grim Reapers. All of them looked at me with some sort of relief, almost as if they were happy to not get stuck watching me.

I stared downwards, not wishing to see the Grim Reapers gazing at me. I nearly crashed into Sumiko's back when she stopped before a huge, musty library. I gaped in awe at the huge shelves lined with books and scrolls of all ages. At the very top was a glass dome that made the room seem even larger.

I sat down at an oak table and Sumiko pulled out a rather old book titled *Order of the Beings*.

"I was informed that Stefan Desmodus showed you most of the Other Realm, yes?"

"Yeah," I answered remembering all the strange and obviously fake things I had seen.

"Alright then. Knowing Stefan, he probably didn't explain much about the creatures you saw, so I will do that now."

I listened as she read aloud to me. According to the book, God was the first being, followed by humans who were made in his image, followed by angels who had no free will, who were then followed by Grim Reapers who had once been human but had been chosen before birth to become what they were now, who were then followed by most other supernatural creature, like hybrids, vampires, and werewolves, and fairies.

I found it funny that something like a vampire was in the same category as a fairy.

Finally, demons came last. The book agreed with what Anthony had told me about them being fallen angels who formed contracts with humans to get their souls, and if no contract could be formed, they would take it by force.

When we had finally finished reading about things I could have read on some phony website, I told Sumiko, "I don't believe in any of this."

She sighed and adjusted her pink cardigan. "Just treat it like some mythology course then. Simply pay attention in case there is a test!"

I liked that perspective. It would be easier if I treated it that way, it would make everything more light-hearted. It wouldn't matter in the end, since everything was a messed up dream.

A beep came from Sumiko's satchel. She pulled out her tablet. "Oh, looks like I've got to pay Robert Smith's soul a visit soon!"

"Don't say that like it's normal!"

She laughed. "It's normal to me!" Her laughter faded off and she stared at the door. "I'll wait until Matthias gets here."

"Who's Matthias?" I asked.

"Matthias Asther is one of the other Grim Reapers that's been assigned to you."

"Seriously?" I didn't think that it was necessary to have me under surveillance 24/7!

The door creaked open and a blonde haired young man crept in. He wore dark sunglasses and a dark green collared shirt.

Sumiko hurriedly said good bye to us and left me with the stoic Matthias Asther.

Chapter 8

There was an a long silence as I sat at the table and Matthias leaned against the door.

I tried to break the silence. "Um, hi..."

"Hello," he responded and made no move to say anything else.

"So, are you Matthias Asther?" I asked stupidly.

He scowled. "Don't ask questions you already know the answers to, boy." He sat across from me and crossed his arms.

I detected some sort of German/Nordic accent from him, but I felt uncomfortable asking him.

"What did Miss Wakahisa tell you?"

"She read to me from a book called the *Order of the Beings*."

"Good," said Matthias. He began to pull out a mini black book from one of his pockets but stopped and put it back in. "I was going to show you some Bible verses and stories about demons, but that would be foolish. It would be more practical to instruct you on how to defend yourself from them."

I smiled at the idea. If I could learn self defense against those monsters, I wouldn't have to rely on these 'Grim Reapers' and I wouldn't be useless.

As we left the library and went through the labyrinth of hallways to get out back, I thought about the people who were watching me. Stefan, Anthony, Sumiko, and Matthias seemed to have known each other, but that was most likely because they were co workers. I had yet to meet the last one.

Behind the Gothic cathedral was a large empty field. Matthias told me to stand in the field while he set up a white table and placed some odd items on it. Once he had finished, he called me over to his side.

On the table was a crucifix, a dream catcher, some weird Native American doll, garlic, a jar of holy water, salt, crystals, some talisman/amulet things, a Bible, some herbs and matches, oil, a guardian angel figure, a picture of Jesus Christ, a statue of the Virgin Mary, a pentagram, paper describing imagining a white light or good aura, and an Eye of Horus.

Matthias gestured to all of it. "These items have been used as protection from monsters, such as vampires and werewolves, or annoying and mischievous beings, such as fairies. Against demons, all of these are said to work..."

I grinned at the sheer amount of items that I could use for protection. I didn't plan on the crucifix or the Virgin and Jesus to be helpful, but everything else could be useful.

The blonde Reaper stood by with a strange smile that seemed out of place. "Too bad that all of this, is in fact useless, and will only attract demons even more."

"Why would you get my hopes up?!" I yelled at Matthias. So much for being able to protect myself. I felt more defenseless than ever.

Matthias smirked at my outburst. "Listen, Oliver. Demons are very powerful. All of these items are linked to the occult in one way or another, even the Bible, because nowhere does it say to use it as protection from demons. Humans can't do much against dark forces unless they are real Christians. That is why you need to be protected. Grim Reapers are experts in exorcisms, because it can be difficult to properly collect a soul to guide to Heaven or Hell with a demon nipping at your heels."

I felt my anger rising. He was like the polar opposite of Sumiko's and Anthony's kindness. "Well," I asked, "What can I do? There has to be at least one thing!"

Matthias pondered my question. "For one thing, don't summon demons or use Ouija or angel boards, but I'm certain that you already know that."

I *really* didn't like Matthias. Even my brother Arthur was more likeable than him. For the first time ever, I actually missed Arthur.

"Another thing that you could do, Oliver, is to not visit places were bloody deaths or murders happened. Demons like those kinds of areas."

"Got it." It wasn't like I could go to any of those places, because there didn't seem to be any in the Other Realm, but I couldn't also because I was being watched like a hawk.

He continued. "Never use witchcraft or any form of magic, especially if you want to hurt someone with it. Demons will also want to attack when you're weak, mentally or physically. If you're drunk or emotional, that will also draw in demons."

I wasn't going to use witchcraft at all, considering what had been going on, and hopefully I would not get sick. One thing was for certain, I would not get drunk.

"Lastly, don't anger a demon on purpose."

"I'll do my best," I said half-heartedly. The information was too much to absorb. There was so much that I couldn't do or else I'd be in danger, and knowing my luck I'd end up doing one of the things. "Is there anything else?"

"Yes, there is." Matthias randomly cringed as though something terrible had happened and quickly jumped to the other side of me.

An olive skinned girl around my age had poked him in the back. Matthias shouted at her. "Luna, never touch me!"

The girl laughed hysterically. "Your personal space issues are entertaining, Asther."

Matthias scowled. "Shut up!" He said to both me and her, since I had laughed at the sight of his panicked face.

The girl called Luna extended her hand for a handshake. "I'm Luna Cortez-Valencia!"

I shook her hand. "I'm Oliver Ravensdale."

"Yes, I've heard about you. What more can you expect from little children?"

"What do you mean by little children?" Luna was obviously childish from the way she messed with Matthias, yet she was calling me a little child.

Luna laughed at me. "Ravensdale, I'm a Grim Reaper! I'm older than your grandparents!"

Matthias leered at her. "You're still a young Reaper, Luna."

Luna's face changed to anger in less than a second. "So, Asther? You're only about twenty years older than I am!"

I stood there, confused, as they argued with each other. If Luna was older than my grandparents, she must be around a century old, and Matthias was older than that! Did they not age at all? I wondered if they stayed the same age as when they died, and I didn't have any better theory.

The two Grim Reapers remembered my presence and stopped fighting. Matthias tried to put back on his stoic expression, but failed due to his left eyebrow twitching. "Anyway, what are you here for, Luna?"

"I finished with my To Die," she paused to chuckle at her own pun,

"List, so Stefan sent me over here, claiming that I was being 'annoying'."

"Why would he ever call you that?" Matthias asked sarcastically.

I shuddered at the mention of the vampire. He seemed so normal, but really he was nothing but a blood thirsty monster.

"Luna," Matthias gestured for her to get out of the way, "I am trying to tell Oliver some warnings about demons, and if you wouldn't interrupt us, it would be very helpful."

She shrugged. "Anything is better than listening to your voice, Asther." She went and sat near the edge of the field.

Matthias seemed relieved to have her out of the way and continued as before. "You shouldn't ever face this problem, but if a demon is trying to possess you, think of things or people you love. Demons are disgusted by feelings of pure love, and that will hold them off enough for at least a little while."

How could I feel such a nice and good emotion in the presence of such evil and ugly creatures? I never thought that it would be so difficult to hold off demons. Actually, it had never crossed my mind.

"Did you get that all in your head, Oliver?"

"Yeah, I guess. It's all too complicated."

He began to put all the items away when Luna called out, "Give Ravensdale the silver cross! Desmodus told me that he ran into some issues with the vampires and a werewolf!"

I was grateful that I had something to defend myself with, but I had no pockets big enough to hold the cross in. Luckily Luna produced a plastic bag from her pocket.

"I found it on my route today," she said to explain why she had a plastic bag in her muddy working jeans.

Matthias was about to respond but his sunglasses slid to the bridge of his nose, showing that his eyes were frozen in fear. Luna froze too, and looked at something behind me. I turned to see what they were staring at, and saw something terrible.

It was a boy, maybe in his late teens, wearing all black. There was nothing wrong with that. What was terrifying were his all black eyes. There were no whites, no iris, no pupils.

He asked me, "I need help. Can you help me?"

Luna pulled me behind her. "Don't answer the demon."

"I need his help," the boy pressed in a smooth yet commanding voice. Matthias stepped up to him. "What do you need, demon?"

The boy was unfazed. "I need his help."

"He can't help you."

"He NEEDS to come with me, so that he can help me," the boy said, slightly angered.

To my great horror, I wanted to listen to him, I wanted to go with him and help him. Fortunately, Luna started to drag me away towards the cathedral.

The black eyed boy seemed infuriated. "No! I need his help! He must be collected!"

Luna and I ran quickly to get away from it. Matthias pulled an ebony scythe from thin air. "In the name of Jesus Christ, go back to Hell."

The boy stubbornly refused. He glanced at a watch on his wrist. "Forget it. It's too late now."

From inside, Luna and I watched as the boy began to leave. I felt a cold sweat break out on me when his lifeless eyes met mine.

In my head I heard his voice. He said, "We will return, Oliver." The boy turned around and vanished.

Chapter 9

Matthias came back inside and took me back to the library, claiming that we could not risk another encounter. Meanwhile, Luna left to report what had happened to her supervisor named Abel.

"What was that thing?" I asked Matthias. "I saw you and Luna responding to it like a demon, but it didn't look like one."

Matthias stared at the table, playing with his glasses. "It was a Black Eyed Child, another form demons can take. Demons can appear as gruesome monsters, heavenly angels, normal people, animals, shadows...anything."

That made everything worse. Who could I trust? Even the Grim Reapers could be demons in disguise. The Angel of Death wasn't exactly good and heavenly looking. I wouldn't doubt for a second that Stefan was a demon. I just wanted to wake up. This is what people in a coma must feel. Being in another world, not being able to wake up to reality. Maybe I was in a coma.

"It was a demon that was sent to collect you. It was hypnotizing you, so that you would go with it, and it would kill you, and take your soul to Hell."

I too stared at the table, not knowing what to say. If ever I would have found myself alone with an actual demon, I'd have been a goner for sure.

"Demons are expert hypnotists," Matthias added. "They're even better than vampires! And that's something. No human can resist the pull of vampires' violet or blue eyes, with swirling golden streaks moving in a circular motion. That's how they get people to feed on."

Since we had moved on to the subject of vampires, I decided to ask about something that had been bugging me. "Why did Stefan run from me? Anthony said that I was a blood source, but isn't he supposed to be protecting me, not leaving me behind while he runs off?"

Matthias nodded like he had heard the story of the old blood sucker that ran from a small human. "Stefan Desmodus is a vampire, and he needs to drink blood. He has had no time to feed since you came, as he was the one who bandaged you and checked on you while you slept. Then he had to show you around, so by the time you made it back here, Stefan was very hungry. And a hungry vampire is brutal and savage, knowing no laws or moral boundary. So he got away from you, or he would've taken every last drop of blood from you. I'm sure that he's fine now."

"That's nice," I said awkwardly. Danger lurked in every corner, and I seemed to run into those corners to often. Soon my luck would run out.

It was getting late, and the library was losing light. Matthias lit a candle, and it became the only light in the room.

Luna and Sumiko came in with candles of their own. Sumiko brought some joyful news. "The Angel of Death has been ordered to confer with Satan, so that perhaps he may call off his demons."

The news became meaningless as Luna scoffed. "It's useless. The devil has never called his demons off on any other human, and Ravensdale won't be the exception!" Before Matthias or Sumiko could scold her, she dismissed herself. "I've got more dead people to collect."

Matthias told Sumiko about the Black Eyed Child. She immediately crushed me in a bear hug.

"Poor little boy! You must be so traumatized!"

I wrenched myself free from the death hug and frowned. "I'm not traumatized." I know that it was a lie, but I wasn't going to let them think that I was even weaker than I was. "This isn't real! It's just a lucid dream. People have been traumatized by them before. They always seem real, but it's nothing but their mind being overactive!"

The two Grim Reapers looked at me pityingly. Matthias sighed. "It's better that you think that way. If you knew this was reality, you would eagerly accept death." He left the room.

Sumiko ruffled my hair. "Ignore what he said. Matthias has always been pessimistic."

"I can tell."

She sat down next to me and stared off into space. It was then that I remembered Luna and Matthias saying that they were more than a century old. I decided to ask Sumiko's age. "How old are you?"

Sumiko thought for a while. "Since I was born in...1928...I am eighty-five years old!"

I stared at her in shock. She was so old! Nothing in her appearance or behavior gave it away.

She laughed at my surprise. "For a Grim Reaper, I'm not that old!"

"I really can't wrap my brain around that." Were Grim Reapers immortal? Or did they just have an extended life? I thought to myself that if didn't matter how long they lived, if they were actually demons. This was all too confusing.

"Oliver," said Sumiko, "Of the four Grim Reapers that have been assigned your case, I'm the second youngest. Anthony is not as old as I am, Luna is second oldest, and Matthias is the oldest."

The library was eerily lit with only two candles. Our faces were cast in a spooky orange light. I thought about the four Reapers. They all seemed to know each other well. I wasn't sure that they were all friends, seeing how Matthias and Luna treated each other, but they were all familiar. Well, in the end it didn't matter.

I moved on to a more pressing matter. "What can actually be done about the demons? When can I go home, or you know, wake up?"

Her face tightened. "The Angel of Death has been sent to investigate. Nothing else can be done at the moment."

Once more, I felt myself grow angered. "Do you expect me to sit around until the demons give up or something? When will that happen? I bet that none of you are doing anything!"

"Oliver, please calm down-"

"How can I calm down? Didn't that book *Order of the Beings* say that Grim Reapers sometimes reveal themselves to people who are about to die? Is that why I've been brought here? So that you can rub it in my face that my case is hopeless?" I had stood from my chair while I had been ranting and I slowly lowered myself back down. "I don't want to die."

Sumiko's eyes were watering at that point. "Gosh, Oliver. Nothing in your world is immortal, everyone will die eventually."

"Yeah, thanks for the words of encouragement," I answered her sarcastically.

"I'll take you to your room," she said as she rose from the table. "I'll leave you by yourself."

I didn't argue with her. I had almost made the girl cry, so I said nothing.

We left the dark library with candles in hand, down the long corridor and to the room that had been labeled mine.

Sumiko left me, promising to return later. I sprawled myself out on the bed, thinking.

If this really was a dream, why could I not wake up? It seemed like an eternity ago I had complained about being in my warm and safe home with my two siblings. My heart ached with that feeling of wanting to cry, but no tears would come out.

If there was a God, why did He allow this mess to happen? I hadn't done anything to deserve what was happening.

I blamed Richard. He was the one who brought the Ouija board and convinced me to play along. He should be the one being hunted down by demons and kept under the watch of Death bringers. Maybe even Edward should be the one suffering, just because he stood there out of harm's way and didn't try to convince me to not play.

I knew it was bad to think that way. No one deserved this. It wasn't really anyone's fault, or was it?

I glared angrily at the bloody crucifix with a bloody Jesus hanging on the wall. Hadn't that Jesus died to defeat the devil? Here I was, about to die at the hand of the devil's minions. What had gone wrong?

At that moment Sumiko came back with a tray of food and saw that I was glaring at her beloved savior. She shook her head and set the tray before me. "Eat or you'll get weak, Oliver. Don't think too hard on the situation, it won't solve anything, okay?" She left again, the door closed with a hard thud.

I slowly spooned around the bowl of soup. I was too worried to want to eat, but my gut told me otherwise.

After I had finished eating I took my bandages off to find fading, pink scars. I looked at the cotton on the bandages, which were tinted yellow. It must have been good medicine.

I sat there on the bed, staring off into space. Everything seemed hopeless.

I was about to fall asleep when there was a knock at the door.

Chapter 10

Anthony entered with a change of clothing for me and a towel. "Kid, we won't have you all dirty and smelling' forever! I'll show you where you can wash."

"Sure." I self consciously sniffed at my shirt. It smelled like dirty socks and sweat. A shower would be a nice thing, especially since it is a great place to just daydream.

We went to Anthony's room, which he shared with a friend of his named Rory who had been out working.

There was a bathroom in the room, and I made sure to lock the door before I showered.

While I showered, I thought of scenarios of how everything could play out, mainly ending in me dying one way or another, only to find that I was dreaming the whole time, and was still in my bedroom at home.

The clothing that had been left for me were all white. I figured that it had something to do with the Reapers' superstitions, but I ignored them. The fabric was thin and cool, like a bed sheet. It was comfortable, and it distracted me for a while.

I left the bathroom to find a red-headed man reading a newspaper.

Anthony wasn't anywhere in the room.

The man saw me standing there not knowing what to do. "Lad, take a seat. Anthony will be back soon."

I obeyed and sat down in a corner.

The man, who I took to be Rory, spoke up. "I'm glad that I didn't get stuck with ya! Hahaha, you've sure got yourself in some trouble! You being here reminded us of some of the other poor souls like you. I once had one, a young girl called Lisa. The idiot chickened out and signed the contract with the demons, lost all the respect we had for her."

It was embarrassing to know that I was being talked about. I was like a hot potato that everyone tossed around and hoped not to get stuck with. Unlucky team of five that got stuck with me.

Lisa had sold her soul, just to stop all the trouble. I wondered if it was worth it in the end. Perhaps it would be easier to just give in. This was all a dream after all.

Rory didn't say anything else, and I silently sat in my corner. Anthony came back a lifetime later. He said to me, "Let's take you back to your room, kid."

We walked in a single file line along many Grim Reapers of all nationalities and all myths drifted past us. It seemed that there were many souls to be collected, so many lives that ended. Would I be among them?

I bumped into people's arms and shoulders for a few minutes, then we finally made it to my room.

Anthony clapped his hands together. "Well, boy, you ain't dying of hunger and smell nice and clean. Try to sleep a little. Sweet dreams. May God and His angels protect you."

"You too..."

He turned to leave. "I'll be patrolling the area, so if anything happens I or someone else will be right around the corner."

"Alright." I closed the door swiftly and crawled under the fluffy covers on the bed.

I couldn't sleep at first, and the reason was understandable. Still, I was tired, and it was a relief to lie down where I felt safe and warm. It was unsettling to know that if the Reapers didn't have so much knowledge about the demons, that one could pop up next to me, and kill me.

A sudden thought came to me. An idea formed in my head. Maybe if I fell asleep, I would proceed to wake up in the real world. I would wake up in my own bed, the one I had had since I very little. I would stay at home to see my parents arrive from work, Father in the afternoon, and Mother in the evening. I would be annoyed and jealous of my big brother. I would get bothered by my little sister's many questions, but answer them anyway. I'd take a break from my friends for a while, after all I had spent nine months of my life every year with them.

With that in mind, I closed my eyes, and fell into a deep -thankfully- dreamless slumber.

When I woke up, the clouds outside were light and white, like in December. I groaned. The idea hadn't come true, for I was still in the Other Realm. I searched the room to see if I could find the time, but there was no clock.

The door burst open, making me jump in surprise. I watched as Luna waltzed in with breakfast. "You like to sleep in late, yes Ravensdale?"

"How did you know I was awake?" I asked her suspiciously.

"Ravensdale, you make more noise than a dog when a stranger is visiting! How could I not hear you?"

I didn't think that I had made much noise at all, but then again, this girl wasn't human. "What time is it?"

"Let's see. It is the same as noon back on Earth!"

"I woke up that late?"

Luna pulled a chair over to the bed. "Yes, but it is better that you spend more time unconscious. That way you aren't scared so much."

"I'm not that scared." I protested.

Her red eyes rolled in disbelief. "Yesterday, or in your time, a second ago, you looked like frightened kitten during a storm! Now, not as much, but still shaken."

"Whatever," I said, eating the waffles on my plate.

There was a long silence. Luna tugged at a loose strand of hair, narrowing her eyes at something in the distance. Eventually, she said me, "Ravensdale, there is some bad news I must tell you."

"What is it?" I asked, thinking of all the dreadful things that could have happened.

"The Angel of Death returned from his meeting with Satan while you slept."

"And?"

"We've gotten nowhere, as I predicted. That devil had the nerve to say, 'The more souls down in Hell the merrier!'"

I lost my appetite and shoved away the remaining waffle. "It was a waste of time."

"Yes it was. But do not fear, we will get the situation under control."

"How can you say that? You've all said something along those lines, and

I really doubt that you can get the situation under control! Do you even know how it'll turn out?"

Luna grinned. "More or less."

My anger flared. I hated Luna. I hated Matthias. I found it harder to hate Anthony and Sumiko, but I still disliked them. I hated all the Grim Reapers. I hated all the freaks in this retarded realm. "Why do you do nothing then? Shouldn't you know what to do? At least tell me what will happen!"

She raised her arms up in defense. "Hold on, Ravensdale. I don't know exactly how this will play out, but I do know how it will end."

"Can't you at least tell me that?" I begged her.

"Sorry, but that's classified information." She leaned forward slightly. "But I can assure you that you'll make it out alive."

I quit talking and silently fumed. I could trust a Grim Reaper to know whether or not a person would die. That was all that I would be able to know, and not knowing exactly what would happen bothered me.

Luna removed the tray from my lap and set it on the floor. "Some demons showed up last night, and attempted to break in."

I didn't answer her, but I acted as though I was ignoring her. I guess that she knew that I was curious, because she continued.

"The Angel took care of it. With his scythe, he gracefully destroyed most of the demons, sending the remainder badly hurt as a warning."

I cocked an eyebrow at Luna's face full of admiration. I mentally laughed at the notion that she liked the head Reaper.

Luna caught on to what I was thinking, and punched me on the arm. "No, no, no, Ravensdale! I just wish that I could be strong enough to beat a horde of demons on my own, but I'm not that strong at all."

"Sure," I said only to annoy her, as revenge for making me angry.

She stuck her tongue out at me but said nothing back.

The Angel of Death truly was powerful, and who wouldn't want to have that kind of power? He wasn't powerful enough because he still needed helpers to collect the hundreds of dead people each day.

According to what the *Order of the Beings* said, people of any nationality could become a Grim Reaper, but only a few who had been chosen before they had been born. Most of them died unnatural deaths, but not all. There was one thing I couldn't understand about them.

I asked Luna, "How do you collect a soul?"

She answered, "We always show up right before a mortal dies. They can never see us unless we choose to reveal ourselves, and that doesn't happen that often. As they lay dying, we touch the center of their forehead and the soul leaves the body. Then, using our scythe to reap it from the air before it escapes and becomes a ghost, we guide it to Heaven or Hell."

"What happens if it becomes a ghost?"

"In that case, the Angel collects the ghost, for they are very difficult to catch."

I found it hard to believe that so many things happened in our world. It all sounded like a stupid story posted online because no one in their right mind would publish it!

Luna began to poke me. "Okay, I need to collect my list of souls for today, and everyone seems to be busy, so you are coming with me."

Seeing as though she gave me no choice, I put on my sneakers which looked dark and dirty in contrast to my white attire.

We went down the elevator and out the lobby, where the ladies at the desk gave me sympathetic smiles before they returned to their work.

Luna and I entered a building that said, "North and Central America". There a Native American man greeted us.

He spoke to Luna. "I had started to think that you had forgotten to come again."

"It's hard to forget after following the same routine for a hundred years."

The man handed her a long list. She seemed surprised. "Why so many?

This is triple the amount of souls I usually have!"

"I'm sorry," said the man, "Mr. Fuqua and Ms. Voslar went rogue. Mortifer told me to assign their work to you, Ms. Cortez."

Luna became furious, and I was beginning to think that she was slightly bipolar. "I already have enough work, in case he hasn't noticed! There's no need to give me more!"

"There is nothing I can do about it."

She stormed out, nearly pulling my arm from its socket. She sat fuming on the cathedral steps. "Idiots..." she muttered to herself.

I stood a few feet away, not wanting to have her let out her anger on me. "Why did this Mortifer choose you, and not someone else? You could tell him that you can't do it."

"I can't do that, Ravensdale. Orders are orders. We must do as we are commanded, unless we want to lose our free will, like Fuqua and Voslar will soon."

"What does that mean?"

"It means that if we disobey, we will be stripped of our ability to choose for ourselves. We will become the perfect servant."

"That's unfair," I said.

Luna stood. "Life is unfair, but whining gets one nowhere."

We went inside. "Okay," Luna said to me, "I've got to start on this huge list, so somebody's gonna have to watch you."

"Who?" I asked.

"Let's see who's available."

She walked up to the indigo eyed woman at the desk. "I've got work to do. Who is able to watch the human for me?"

The woman checked her computer. "Mr. Asther, Mr. Griffin, and Ms. Wakahisa are all busy. Mr. Desmodus is free though, I'll give him a call. Please wait here."

Luna and I sat in the waiting area, and I began to get nervous at the thought of being alone with Stefan. I hoped that he had drank some blood, because I didn't want to become a supplier.

The vampire came in with a glass of what seemed to be blood. "Luna, what did you need?"

"I need you to watch Ravensdale for a bit."

"Oh, of course. I'll keep him safe and sound."

Luna walked out, and called back, "Don't go sucking his blood, Desmodus."

He smiled. "I'll try to restrain myself."

Chapter 11

I freaked out internally as Stefan stood before me.

He seemed to know that I was scared, and laughed at me. "Relax, Mr. Ravensdale!" He took a swig of his drink. "I can assure you that I have enough blood to keep me satisfied for a long while."

"That's reassuring." Not really at all, but it was nice to know that I wouldn't be in any in any trouble from Stefan, at least not for some time."

Stefan sat next to me, stroking his goatee. "So much has happened to you, I do not understand how you haven't gone insane."

"Maybe I have gone insane, and that's why all this is happening in my head."

He shook his head. "No, I don't think it is all in your head."

"Whatever." It didn't matter what he thought, I just hoped that the nightmare would end quickly.

The lobby emptied out, and all that could be heard was the quiet chatter of the secretaries.

April Padalecki ran through the doors with a tall, brown haired man that resembled her. They spoke to the secretaries in hushed tones.

I tried my best to listen, but I couldn't catch a thing. Fortunately Stefan could.

"They wish to speak with the Angel of Death over something important...something concerning you, Mr. Ravensdale."

Almost on cue, April and her companion looked my way.

I supposed that the guy was also a werewolf, and maybe that he was April's father or brother. The two of them were allowed entry and were escorted by the fat secretary to the elevator.

"Wait, if they have to say something about me, shouldn't I go too?"

Stefan laid his hand on my shoulder, it was cold. "If you are needed, Mr. Ravensdale, you will be sent for."

Time passed, and I felt that a clock needed to be there to tick tock the moments away. Four Grim Reapers that I had never seen before came down and waited at the door. Then my Grim Reapers came down. They handed their Soul Lists to the Reapers at the doors and then quickly filed into the elevators.

"Why did they do that, Stefan?"

Stefan frowned. "The news the wolves brought must be urgent for them to be sent for. I'm sure that they'll call for you any moment now."

Just as he predicted, a secretary spoke to me. "Oliver, sweetie, please go up to Death's office."

Stefan and I did so, and entered the dark angel's quarters. I was worried, and wondered what might have happened.

In the office, Matthias paced, Anthony and Sumiko conversed anxiously, Luna sat with her head in her hands, and the two werewolves were standing off to the side with nervous expressions.

The Angel of Death, in the midst of everything, reclined in his chair, seemingly relaxed. "Oliver, sit down. There is an important issue that we must discuss."

I stood there, not knowing what would happen, but I moved forward and obeyed the angel after Stefan shoved me forward.

"W-what happened?" I asked Death.

"The demons have devised a new scheme. They have taken your family and those two children, Edward Jones and Richard Stevenson, as hostages," Death answered.

Everyone that I actually cared about, were prisoners of those terrible things that had tormented me so often in my dreams. This one, by far, was the worst. "What do they want with them?"

"The demons want to form a contract for your soul, and in exchange they will deliver your loved ones back to safety, with no memory of the demons or any other creature they may have seen. If you refuse, they will take their souls by force, and then hunt you down in the worst way possible."

"But what about Edward? He believes in all this stuff."

"Yes, him. The demons despise him for his fear of God, and so plan to torment and torture him, until his body and mind cannot take anymore, and die."

None of this could be real...none of this was actually happening...this was nightmare, and nothing more...I would just play along. "Prove it. How do you know for sure that the demons have them as their captives?"

April held out Edward's cross and Samantha's toy pony. "My brother, Logan, and I found these dropped in our territory."

Logan nodded. "The demons must have sent someone else to do the dirty work, most likely a goblin or a dwarf, because there were traces of smaller, but strong people." He showed me a yellowed piece of paper. "Our Alpha and other elders caught a demonic scent stuck to those to items. We called upon Morgan le Fay to find out what happened and she recorded what she discovered on here."

I took both the paper and the items. This had to be true, for Ed always wore his cross since he was little, and Sam loved the pony to pieces. It was the last present our Grandma gave her before she passed away.

I tried to blink away the tears that were forming in my eyes. I needed to be strong, I wouldn't let the demons get the best of me. "What will you do about this?" I asked Death.

He smiled creepily. "I can't do anything."

"Nothing?" I exclaimed in outrage.

"Nothing at all."

"You can't be serious!"

Matthias stopped pacing. "He is dead serious, Oliver."

"But they'll be killed!" I protested.

Death continued to grin from under his hood. "This too happened for a reason."

What was wrong with this so called angel? How could this happen for a reason? I no longer cared if this was fact or fiction, I couldn't take anymore of this. If there was a God, He hated my guts. "What will happen if you don't do anything?"

"You shall discover that, Oliver," Death responded.

That was the last straw. I ran from the room. I didn't know which floor my room was on, and I couldn't go to the bottom floor without the secretaries stopping me. Thus I ignored the elevator and huddled in a far corner under another stained glass window, one depicting Christ sweating blood, looking up to the sky, and leaning on a large rock.

"He was scared, and worried. He didn't want to die, but He did it for the good of all of us. Because He loved us so much that He gave up His mortal life,"said Anthony.

"Why did He do that? Isn't He supposed to be some powerful god?"

Anthony sat down beside me. "He was human at the same, and it was the only way to save us."

"I see," said I, but I didn't care at all. "Anthony, how can the Angel of Death not do anything about this? Isn't he supposed to protect me?"

"I'm not sure, kid. He didn't tell us anything besides what you were told."

I looked at the cross and pony, and for the first time the tears were let loose. I hated not being able to do anything. I wanted to do something, but I had no idea what. Dream or not, I could not stand the idea that all the important people in my life were in danger. Without them, I had no one.

"Can I go back to my room?" I asked Anthony.

"Sure, kid. You must be stressed out."

"Of course I am."

"Everything will be fine. I promise."

His attempt to reassure me slipped in through one ear and exited out the other. Everything would not be fine, and no one was able to promise anything.

In the elevator, I memorized all the floor numbers, with a plan forming in my head.

I was not going to lay back and do nothing like that useless angel. I had to put myself to work.

Chapter 12

The minute that I got to the room and Anthony departed, I shoved the cross and pony into the plastic bag with the silver crucifix.

I took a moment to thoroughly read Morgan le Fay's report. It read about the demons' threats and conditions, but it also revealed where my family and friends were being kept. They were in the Fairy Village, in the mountains, the place Stefan warned me against visiting.

Apparently if I asked the dwarf guards for the dwarf chief, he would take me to my family and Edward and Richard. There the demons would wait to make the contract with me.

Yes, I planned to sell my soul. I didn't have any form of heroic plan. We would leave and live like we used to, and no one except for me would remember the events. The only obstacle I had was to go out unnoticed.

I clutched the bag closely and silently opened the door. Thankfully the hallway was empty, the doors were all closed, and no one was using the elevator. It occurred to me that the elevator would give me away, so I took the winding stairs next to it. I braced myself for the long descent, since I was on the fourth floor.

Easily I grew tired, and I wasn't sure on what level I was on. The only noise that reached me was my exhausted breathing and footsteps.

At the bottom of the stairs, I reached a door. I pushed it, but then I found that I had to pull it inwards. I cautiously peered out and saw Sumiko talking to one of the secretaries. I would not be able to sneak out without her or a secretary taking notice of me.

I then remembered that there was a back door. It had been the one I had gone through when Matthias thought he had been giving me helpful tips.

I heard Sumiko enter the elevator. I sneaked out of the door and tried to hurry into the long hall next to it. At the far end there was a window that looked out into the empty field.

The tallest of the secretaries saw me. "Where are you going?" She asked in a Jersey accent.

"Oh, uh, Matthias Asther wanted to teach me some self defense outside."

The secretary seemed unconvinced. "Let's see if Mr. Asther is here at the moment."

I stood there, hoping that he hadn't gone out soul collecting. I frowned. I could have come up with a better excuse.

She waved me off. "Yeah, he's here. Now go on, no need to distract me from my work."

Relieved, I dashed down the hall, the white clothing fluttered behind me.

I was completely out of breath by the time I burst out the door and was greeted by the smell of death.

Briefly I stayed there, remembering my way to the fairies. It was simple, since I had gone out from behind the cathedral, I didn't have to go through the vampires, but I would have to hurry out into either the gardens or the mushrooms. I wondered how I'd get past the pixies, but that was an issue I'd have to face later.

I nearly had a heart attack when the back door opened. Matthias came out, glaring at me sternly. "Oliver Ravensdale, you had the nerve to lie about training so that you could run off?"

I said nothing. I should have counted on the secretaries alerting him that I was outside.

"What were your intentions, boy?"

I was ashamed to tell him, but I knew that he'd get the answer one way or another. I replied, "I was going to the dwarfs and the demons, to exchange my soul for my family."

He growled at me. "Seriously? You're that dim-witted? Do you think that those demons have even a shred of mercy? They would have taken your soul, and then your loved ones' as well! That is, if some monster didn't get to you first!"

His words stung, but I knew that he was right. There was no way that I would be able to manage on my own. It was ridiculous, and I needed help. "In that case, will you help me?"

"Don't even consider that a possibility," Matthias answered. "There is too much risks, and I would be severely punished for interfering with the matters of life and death of people I'm not supposed to protect."

I bitterly said, "Every single person here is a heartless monster." I knew that I was being unfair, but that did not matter in the slightest. All the people that I had always taken for granted were in danger, and I couldn't let them die, whether the events were part of reality or a horrible nightmare.

Matthias pushed his sunglasses up in a condescending manner. "You may be right, Oliver. But what can be done? To be frank, I wish that God would've let the demons have you, instead of putting us on guard duty and bringing more humans in danger, including an innocent believer."

I hung my head at his harsh words. Was that what everyone thought? Were their kindness and smiles fake? Was I just an annoying human who didn't deserve to live?

He continued, "I follow God's orders, and it is clear that it is not your time to die yet. It is in your best interest to stay here, unless you'd like to commit suicide by going on your destined to fail quest." Matthias promptly returned indoors, aware that I wouldn't dare to go alone.

I sat on the cold, hard ground. It started to rain, but I didn't want to go inside and face the Grim Reapers who only saw me as a burden.

Too enveloped in my thoughts was I to notice that someone held an umbrella over my head.

"Oliver, please come on inside. You'll catch a cold!"

I noticed Sumiko standing over me, her words charitable in contrast to Matthias' words, but they were most likely fake anyway. "No, I'm fine."

Instead of pulling me inside, she joined me. "What did Matthias say to you? He seemed upset."

I told her what had led to his angry lecture. "I'm sorry that I've caused so much trouble."

"You didn't cause any of what's happening! It's the greedy demons. They treat everyone like their chess pieces, using them to twist the world into their evil dream come true."

The rain kept coming down, showing no sign of slowing. "What will happen to them?" I asked, referring to my parents, siblings, and friends. I already knew the answer, but I wanted to hear it aloud.

Sumiko stood up with an air of determination. "We were never told to not go save your loved ones. Anthony and Luna will help. Stefan won't care at all, and what Matthias doesn't know won't hurt him."

She pulled me to my feet and closed her eyes for a few minutes.

"What are you doing?"

"Grim Reapers can talk to each other with their minds."

"Cool."

Soon, we had been joined by Anthony and Luna.

Anthony had come prepared with his own sack of defenses, and put my bag in it.

Luna wore an oversized red hoodie, claiming that the weather was freezing, which it was not.

I smiled at the three Reapers. Surely they weren't heartless. "So, you'll help?"

"Heck yeah," said Anthony, "I may not agree with your choices, but your heart's in the right place."

Luna agreed. "Family is important after all, and you only live once!"

Anthony rolled his eyes. "We are death, we'll never die."

"Is that a challenge?"

Sumiko smiled but became serious. "Let's get going. We'll need to keep a low profile as we go."

I studied my group. An Asian girl dressed in a pink sweater set, an African American carrying a sack of different weapons and artifacts, and a short Hispanic girl flopping her oversized, red sleeves. It would be hard to go unnoticed.

Chapter 13

We trudged through the rain that blew with the wind. I feared that vampires were roaming about, but Anthony assured me that they preferred Earth over the Other Realm. I didn't fear the were-creatures, for they were far off.

The lands had no noise, it seemed that it was holding its breath, waiting to see the outcome of our mission. Although the fairies were close, the rain made it more difficult to get there.

We speed-walked and kept our eyes forward. It was only after we cleared the Soul Haven and its rain that we took notice that Sumiko was missing, but quickly she caught up with us.

She showed us a small, bronze coin with a pentagram on it. "The demons, or the dwarfs, left this for us. They knew what you would choose, Oliver."

It was odd, to know that I was playing into their game. I dreaded what was to come, but it had to be done. I doubted that I'd make it out alive. I was exhausted, reality blurred with fiction, I wanted to survive.

Anthony said, "Kid, if you want to go back, we can go."

I shivered. The field between Fairy Village and Soul Haven was chilly, and a moon shone brightly over head. This had to end sooner or later, and I wanted to get it over with soon. "No, we can keep going. I won't leave my family behind."

"Good for you, Ravensdale," Luna cheered. "If all goes well, you'll need a lifetime of therapy, but good for you!"

Anthony smacked her on the head. "That's not helping!"

She mimicked him and ran farther ahead.

The silence was ever present, or steps were the only noise makers. I felt watched, but I could see no one besides our group.

In the night, I could see the glowing, unnatural colored eyes of the three Reapers. I was grateful that they had risked punishment to help me, and resented Stefan and Matthias for being so cowardly. They preferred to stay on Death's good side than help save innocent lives.

The field was large, and I wished we could fly over it, like Stefan and I did. The night ceased to be silent, loud barking and growling sounded in the distance. I guessed that the werewolves were out hunting.

Luna, who had been running a good distance ahead of us, didn't think so. She held up her scythe, and came to us.

"What is it?" Sumiko asked, scared.

"Hell hounds," said Luna. "Obviously they wanted Ravensdale alone, and we're uninvited company."

"Hell hounds?" I said, puzzled, even though I had heard of them.

Anthony explained. "They're basically the diabolical pets of hell, and some of the more powerful demons."

The were closer, and I could see them. Enormous black dog/wolf things with red eyes and razor like teeth, they were like no creature I had ever seen.

"What are we gonna do?" Sumiko yelled, while she waved her own scythe frantically.

Anthony suggested that they fight them head on.

"No! We can't do that! They'll tear us to shreds!"

I was confused for a moment, when I remembered something from the *Order of the Beings*. Grim Reapers could be killed, but only by the Angel of Death, and the powerful demons. We faced an actual problem that the Grim Reapers couldn't survive.

"Shut up!" Luna angrily shouted. She looked at us in the way a protective adult looked at children in danger of hurting themselves. "Griffin and Wakahisa- there's an abandoned goblin whole, see that, right there- take Ravensdale and hide in it. I'll distract those dogs. When they are all focused on me, QUIETLY sprint across the meadow. Keep in mind that most fairy folk are sleeping, don't disturb. I'll meet up with you later, if God so desires," she mumbled the last part.

I couldn't believe that the girl who had previously been whacking everything with her sleeves had become serious and in control.

We had no time to disagree with Luna's idea because the hellhounds came nearer and nearer. Anthony, Sumiko, and I dashed into the old goblin hole, and I peered over the edge. Luna kept beating the hounds away from us and closer in the direction of the Vampire Coven and the Were Lands. No longer did the hounds focus on taking the good for nothing boy alone, but focused on the pesky Grim Reaper that was hurting them.

I had not done much at all. These people that I hadn't known for a long time at all had gone to great lengths to help me, but I was going to repay them somehow. That is, as soon as I wasn't flung over Anthony's shoulder like a rag doll.

They took off and sprinted, and I watched as Luna and the hounds disappeared over the horizon. Since my companions were not human, they went at much greater speeds. Arthur nor any of his teammates could never have gone as fast.

We stopped once we were in the gardens. Neither Grim Reaper was out of breath, and they scanned the area.

My voice was hardly above a whisper. "She'll be fine, right?"

Sumiko's eyes gleamed with tears, and Anthony shrugged with his face downcast.

A heavy blanket of worry fell over us. I was to blame for this. I should have died days ago. I only brought bad luck to all.

The gardens beheld no crazy, old gnomes or child-like pixies, the statues of weeping angels and Hellenistic people were the only occupants.

We marched on. The toadstool houses of the elves resounded with snores and sluggish breathings, no wonder as they worked all day.

The toadstools ceased to grow, and the grass dried up. The mountains towered into the dark atmosphere. Caves dotted the mounts, and ugly little people wobbled around, the dwarfs. They glowered at us, but kept to themselves.

At the base of the mountain, a huge cave opened its mouth. It was guarded by two dwarf sentries.

"Whatcha want, eh?" grumbled one troll-faced fellow.

I answered him. "I'm Oliver Ravensdale, and I want to see the dwarf chief about my family and friends."

The dwarfs grinned at one another. The one who had spoken first stood aside and motioned for us to enter. "Chief's been expecting' you, human." He nodded to his partner. "Fleegmur here will take you to him."

Fleegmur made sure that we were following him before he led us straight down the corridor into a larger cave. In it, a group of dwarfs sat in a ragged circle, drinking and being rowdy.

Fleegmur called their attention and proclaimed, "Your majesty, the human boy and two of his protectors have arrived!"

An elderly and cruel looking dwarf stood from the head of the circle. He came to me. "You here for you family?"

"Yes, I want to make the exchange."

He roared with laughter. "Ho ho ho! Human- hee hee hee- you're so foolish!"

He turned to Anthony and Sumiko. "You two can't go with him. Stay here."

Anthony stared him down. "We are going with him."

"Too bad-"

"A Grim Reaper can't interfere without a direct order from Mortifer or God, and we have no order," said Sumiko.

I wondered who Mortifer was, but when I put two and two together I realized that was the Angel of Death's name.

"Alright then, girly." He pointed to an off shooting passageway. "Follow straight down, and you'll find what you're looking for."

My feet felt like heavy anchors but I mustered strength to go forward. This was the end, there I died.

Chapter 14

It mattered not that I was flanked by two Death Bringers, for they could only watch anyway.

A sizable cavern opened at the end of the passage. I was filled with terror at the sight of it. The walls were lined with lanterns, which provided most of the light. The rest came from a glowing pentagram on the floor, and it was surrounded by candles.

I felt something touch my neck, something cold and airy. Whatever it was choked me. The demons had made their presence known.

"Oliver Ravensdale...we knew that you would come..."

I stepped back, unsure of where to direct my attention. "Where are they?"

A cage was lowered on a chain to the ground. Father, still in his suit, Mother in her nurse garb, Arthur, Samantha, Edward, and Richard were each bound and unconscious. By their facial expressions, I could see that they were dreaming their worst nightmare.

Instead of the grotesque demons I had seen before, they appeared as shadow people on the walls. I had only seen things like those on paranormal shows.

Before me appeared a long piece of paper and a pen. It read:

Oliver J. Ravensdale, by signing this contract, will give up ownership of his soul and his place in Paradise will cease to exist. In exchange for those two belongings, Michael and Eloise Ravensdale, Arthur Ravensdale, Samantha Ravensdale, Edward Jones, and Richard Smith will be set free with no memory of their ordeal in the Other Realm. Oliver Ravensdale will be allowed to spend the rest of his earthly life with them, as long as he does our bidding. Once signed, he will be damned for all of eternity, and nothing will be able to save him.

Below the text, there was a strange assortment of symbols, and I was not able to recognize any of them. Next to them in an empty space was where I would write my name.

I took the pen in my shaking hand. Anthony and Sumiko could not help me. I was completely alone.

"Go on, human," said a demon, "or they will suffer." It gestured to my family.

I froze in place for years it seemed, thinking about what had led up to this moment, and how I could have avoided it.

Filled with resolve, I set the pen down on the empty spot. I wanted to be the hero, to be able to save those I cared for, but deep in my heart, I knew that I would regret the decision I would make.

I moved the pen slightly, drawing a trail of blood red ink. I hurriedly used the pen to tear the paper in two.

A shadow woman clawed me across the face. Warm blood fell like tears, but I could not wipe them away. "What do you think you are doing, human?"

Another shadow produced another contract. "Give him another chance. I can smell his fear and uneasiness."

I let my guard slip at the second chance given to me by a demon, and I thought that maybe they weren't so bad as everyone made them out to be. Then I recalled what the demons had done to me, and told myself that these creatures had no love or compassion.

My mind wandered to the previous people who had found themselves in the same problem. Would I be like the girl who sold her soul, or be one of those who refused and died honorably?

It seemed that there was nothing that I could do, but I knew that I had one trick up my sleeve. One that no one would expect me to use. It was difficult to manage though.

I pictured everyone I liked throughout my life, and put them where the shadow demons were. Instead of menacing figures, I saw my kind, old neighbors, my favorite teachers, favorite actors, my family, and friends. The warm feelings of love, friendship, and care flowed to the demons, much to their great disgust.

What I did was not enough. I saw all of the shadows take flight, except for the largest one.

It grabbed me and throttled me. "Stupid, midget mortal! I am the Prince of Darkness! I vowed that such petty feelings would never touch me like it did in that war thousands of years ago!

"Few mortals have learned that trick, only one besides you have done it on me. I made certain that he was beheaded by his fellow countrymen. Just imagine your own death!"

"Leave him alone!" Anthony yelled.

The demon sneered at him. "What can you do to help him? Nothing, just like your God."

I was in a full blown panic attack. The only thought process that went through my brain was that I should have signed the paper, I should have signed the contract. I didn't want to die.

In that moment, a glorious light occupied the room. The 'Prince of Darkness' let go of me and cowered from the pure light. In the midst of it, stood a tall, white angelic figure. It had the same porcelain like features of Mortifer. But it wore a white robe and a smile full of lovingness.

The angel spoke to the demon. "By God Almighty's command, retreat to your hellish dominion and plague this guiltless mortal no more. His heart is good and pure, and shall not be tainted by your evil!"

The demon glared hatefully at the angel, but obeyed and left like the rest of the demons.

"Young Oliver," the angel said to me, "have you been terribly injured?"

I checked myself, them stammered, "Only my face has been scratched."

The saving angel helped me to my feet and then healed my face completely. It commanded Sumiko and Anthony to watch me momentarily. From the looks on their faces, I knew that they had not expected the angel to arrive.

My family and two friends had peaceful and happy expressions, for they were no longer affected by the demons.

The angel released their sleeping forms from the cage, and more angels of its kind appeared. Each one carried a person in their arms. I found it strange to see my proud father and brother carried like infants. Mother and Sammy didn't bother me as much, as they looked natural close to beings of the light. Edward seemed joyful, while Richard sleep fought the angel that carried him. The angels departed to return them back home.

I was soon trapped in a death hug by Anthony and Sumiko. They talked about how hard it had been to stand back and watch, even though they had had orders to protect me.

"Well, kid, that was awesome!" Exclaimed Anthony. "Had you planned to use the power of pure emotions, one way to call angels by the way, all along?"

I hung my head in embarrassment. "Not really. I actually planned to sign the contract. I was just winging it at the end."

"Well, that was just plain lucky then!"

We laughed together, and for the first time during those days, I felt content. I hadn't died, and I was done with the demons. I couldn't have asked for more.

The angel that had rescued me reappeared. It explained what they had done. "The Ravensdale family and young Stevenson and Jones have been put into what you call, a nap. When they awaken, they shall not remember the demons or dwarfs at all."

That was a relief. At least they weren't traumatized for life.

"Now, Oliver," said the angel. "You have unfinished business that must be taken care of before you can return to your home."

"What is there left to do?" I asked.

"You have unfinished business in Soul Haven." The angel opened a portal made of blinding light. "Oliver, Mister Griffin, and Miss Wakahisa, please step through here."

Chapter 15

We did as we were told and found ourselves before the dark cathedral. I braced myself for possibly another lecture, and the Grim Reapers did the same.

The secretaries giggled amongst themselves, most likely about Anthony and Sumiko's incoming punishment.

On the way up to Mortifer's office, I wondered why the two Reapers seemed to be in a trance, but then I recalled that they were able to communicate through their brains.

I began to feel bad about them. I hoped that they would not be punished, or worse, have to lose whatever free will they had.

The elevator stopped and we stood outside the office. After a while Anthony timidly knocked, and the door was opened by an angry Stefan.

Inside, Matthias leaned against a pillar, and his face expressed guilt. Luna survived the hell hounds, but had her arm wrapped in bloody bandages. Mortifer sat behind his desk with a pleased grin.

He spoke. "Oliver, I did nothing, and my helpers did nothing in reality, except causing more issues," he referred to the hellhound attack. "You found the solution on your own, like we knew that you would."

"What do you mean?" I inquired.

"My brethren came to help you after you performed the difficult task of expelling the emotions of love and kindness in the presence of demons. You overcame the fear you had, if only for a brief moment, and did the unthinkable. You found the solution."

I sighed in aggravation. It bothered me that Mortifer and his God knew exactly what would've happened. At least the Reapers told me what they could. I held a lot of dislike towards both of them.

Matthias swallowed his pride and said, "Oliver, forgive me for not helping you. It was selfish of me, but I am glad that you took my instructions to heart."

"Yeah, it's fine, Matthias," was all I could say before I turned away.

"See, Ravensdale," said Luna, "it all turned out fine in the end! No one died and you can go back to your regular life!"

Stefan interjected, "You were nearly torn to shreds by those mutts!"

"Relax, Desmodus, it's just my arm! And it'll heal...in a few years."

I was confused as to why Stefan cared, but Sumiko came and explained, "Stefan is in charge of making sure that the younger Grim Reapers don't get hurt. He's like our guardian. Luna getting hurt is the first strike in his otherwise perfect injury free record."

"Oh." I gave the vampire an apologetic look, but he refused to look at me. I said, "When will I be leaving?"

"Right now," responded the Angel of Death. "I must tell you that when we leave this plane, you will fall asleep, and I cannot guarantee that you will have any memory of this."

"It's better that way."

The angel nodded in agreement and opened another blinding portal, and pulled his hood over his eyes, "So that the light wouldn't blind."

Before I stepped through, I wanted to give proper farewells. Anthony patted me on the back. "Don't go messing with demons, okay?"

Sumiko hugged me. "Oliver, I'm happy to let you know that you'll go on to live a long and normal life."

Luna messed with me hair. "Good bye, Oliver. I wonder which one of us will get to visit you one day?"

Stefan shook my hand. "Stay safe, Mr. Ravensdale," was all he said.

Lastly, I said goodbye to Matthias. I was still angry with him for not helping me, but I was grateful for what he had taught me. "Take care," said he. He took a small wooden cross from his pocket. "Take this, so that you may have something to remember us by."

I thanked him and placed the cross in one of the white pants' pockets.

Without glancing back, I stepped through the portal followed by

Mortifer, who carried me when I went to sleep.

Chapter 16

I blinked a few times before I opened my eyes. Green leaves hung over my head. I sat up to find that Richard and Edward were snoring beside me. I had no clue as to why we were sleeping in the forest.

I woke them up, and they had no idea why we were in the forest either. Edward got a call from his mother, saying that we had to return before the rain shower began.

The three of us got up and walked back to Ed's house, where food awaited.

On the way we spoke about sports, and I was utterly lost, but I was happy to be with them all the same.

When we had closed the gate to the forest, Richard stomped his feet. "Oh man! I forgot to show you the surprise!"

"What was it?" Edward asked.

"My sister's Ouija board."

At the mention of it, images of demons, people called Grim Reapers, gnomes, and other paranormal creatures flooded my mind.

I figured that they were just memories from one of my many nightmares, as I was always able to remember most of them.

We went indoors and I shoved my hands into my black sweats' pockets. My hand rammed into a wooden object. I pulled it out and found the small, wooden cross. I was seized with fear, for it meant that the memories had been real, not from a dream land.

I hid it back in my pocket and made sure that no one had seen it.

The three of us ate lunch with Mrs. Jones and Edward's baby sister. When we had finished, we went up to his room and sat in a circle.

I told my two closest friends everything, from the first nightmares to Matthias giving me the cross. In conclusion, I passed them the cross, so that they would see my proof.

Richard sat holding his head. "It hurts my brain! I can't understand this..."

"I'm not sure if you're telling the truth or not," Edward said, "but that is why it is safer to believe in what isn't seen."

I shook my head confused. "I don't know. I mean, there could be paranormal and divine beings, but then again they could just be created from our imaginations."

Epilogue

I never knew what to believe. My entire life was shrouded in confusion. I wanted to believe that the supernatural existed, but I doubted it too much at the same time.

Now, in my advanced years, I still had the tiny, wooden cross. The adventure I lived in the Other Realm, whether it was real or not, never faded from my mind. I relived it many times.

Today, I sat alone in my room, rocking back and forth in a rare antique chair. They didn't make the same furniture as they did before.

I sensed that soon I would leave this cruel world of ours. As the years progressed, our glorious Earth became more corrupt. I would be happy to leave it soon.

The polluted sky darkened, and my eyes began to get heavy. I went to bed, and fell into a deep sleep.

I opened my eyes once more, and nearly had a heart attack. In the darkness, I saw blazing yellow, baby pink, neon green, and blood red eyes. "...Grim Reapers..."

In unison they said, "Oliver Ravensdale, it is time to go to your final destination. Your final resting place."

Author's Note

This story was sparked by all the media surrounding Grim Reapers in all their different cultures. Since I was twelve, I was interested in the different Death figures around the world. For the next year, an idea formed in my head that would serve as the basis for this book.

Originally, I intended Oliver to be a Christian, but later on I decided on making him an Atheist, to make the story more interesting. I never meant to offend anyone, but instead attempted to break the stereotype of Atheists that many Christians have by portraying the Ravensdales as any other family. An athletic sibling, a kind sibling, a smart one, two hard-working parents.

It was a difficulty to write the book as I had issues deciding on which myths were more accurate or what information about demons was more realistic, but in the end I combined many of them with my own theories.

I'd like to thank my family for being here with me through the long process. I'd also like to thank my good friends Emma Pearson, Sarah Sugita, Natalie Stapleton, and Becca Peterson for putting up with me talking about the paranormal nonstop. In addition to them, I'd like to thank the DeviantART community, more specifically my watchers for listening and helping me with the book when I ran into troubles. I also want to thank my teachers at Trinity

My life flashed before my eyes, and I breathed my last, happy. No more did I doubt. In my final moments I believed in what we cannot see.

Lutheran for instructing me all these years.

Most of all, I want to thank my Father. He has blessed me with the ability to create new worlds in simple, English words. I thank Him, for without His ever present love, I would have never found the strength to put my ideas into words. I would die for the sake of my Savior.

Thank you to all who have taken their precious time to read my book. I know that it is not the best, but I'm working hard to improve my skills.

-Diana Montanez-Mendoza

Made in the USA
Charleston, SC
01 September 2013